# JULIE

## *and*

# MONICA

### HOPE BEHIND THE TEARS

**DAVID ALLEN SMITH, M.D.**

Scripture quotations are taken from the Holy Bible, New International Version®, NIV®. Copyright © 1973, 1978, 1984, 2011 by Biblica, Inc.™ Used by permission of Zondervan. All rights reserved worldwide.

WestBow Press books may be ordered through booksellers or by contacting:

WestBow Press
A Division of Thomas Nelson & Zondervan
1663 Liberty Drive
Bloomington, IN 47403
www.westbowpress.com
1 (866) 928-1240

Because of the dynamic nature of the Internet, any web addresses or links contained in this book may have changed since publication and may no longer be valid. The views expressed in this work are solely those of the author and do not necessarily reflect the views of the publisher, and the publisher hereby disclaims any responsibility for them.

Any people depicted in stock imagery provided by Thinkstock are models, and such images are being used for illustrative purposes only.
Certain stock imagery © Thinkstock.

ISBN: 978-1-9736-0485-3 (sc)
ISBN: 978-1-9736-0486-0 (e)

Library of Congress Control Number: 2017914860

Print information available on the last page.

WestBow Press rev. date: 01/02/2018

WestBow
PRESS®
A DIVISION OF THOMAS NELSON
& ZONDERVAN

This book is dedicated to all the families of premature babies that have lived through the highs and lows associated with life in neonatal intensive care units. They have fought alongside the doctors and nurses to preserve and save the most precious commodity of all time – human life.

David A. Smith, MD, FACS

Diplomate of The American Board of Surgery in General Surgery

Diplomate American Board of Surgery with Special Certification in Pediatric Surgery

Director Pediatric Trauma and Transport Lutheran Children's Hospital

Director Perinatal Center Lutheran Children's Hospital

Clinical Faculty Indiana University School of Medicine

Instructor Saint Francis University

Instructor Indiana Wesleyan University

# Preface

It is a tragedy when parents lose a child. My own mother lost a baby to a congenital heart defect at a time when all such babies died. She understood that nothing could be done to save her baby, but the loss still haunts her memory more than sixty years later. My brother survived only a few hours. His grandparents encouraged my mom to not take any photos or even hold him. They did not want her to develop emotional attachments to the baby and thought that limited contact was the best course of action. She followed her parents' advice and did not allow my father, an avid photographer, to take a photo of little Donald David. What they didn't understand was that nine months of pregnancy had already bonded them together. My mom now deeply regrets her decision and wishes she had a photograph. Her only keepsake to remind her of little Donald is a beaded bracelet with his name spelled out in six small blue square letters. Not "bonding" with her baby did not assuage my mother's pain; it only compounded her anguish.

Mothers who carry their babies for as short as a few weeks can build emotional ties even though they do not bond with their babies in the traditional sense. Miscarriage and elective abortion both deprive women of the opportunity to see, feel, and interact with their living babies outside the womb. These women still feel the same kind of sorrow and grief experienced by my mother.

Working in the neonatal intensive care unit, as I do, is very rewarding and frustrating at the same time. Some days it is two steps forward followed by three steps backwards. When babies run out of sites to place an IV (intravenous catheter), the pediatric surgeon is called upon to insert a central venous line. Most commonly the line is placed using a technique called a "cutdown." The surgeon makes an incision over a vein to expose it in order to thread the central venous line into a larger vein.

Over the lifespan of a pediatric surgeon, he or she may be called upon to do hundreds of such surgeries. It was during one of these procedures during my fellowship that I realized that the extreme premie (a child born on the very edge of viability) upon which I was operating was squirming in pain. I had been trained to think that extreme premies don't feel pain; therefore, no local anesthetic had been injected for the procedure. I learned, however, that babies at twenty-one to twenty-three weeks gestation *do* feel pain. Since that incident, I have always used local anesthetic for even the smallest procedures.

The idea for this book came about after a physician who was friends with my wife and I told us a story about his own wife. She was a nurse. Her first job was working in a clinic assisting with abortion procedures. He told us about her experiences. Mid-term and late-term pregnancies were aborted using dilation and extraction. This is a method for extracting babies in pieces. Sometimes the babies were killed first with an injection of digoxin into the amniotic fluid, which slowed or stopped the baby's heart. Mostly, the babies were still alive during the procedure.

The realization came slowly to me at first, but then hit me very hard. The same pain felt by my twenty-one- to twenty-three-week premies was also being felt by those mid-term and late-term aborted babies. This knowledge literally brought me to tears. While we work so hard to save the precious lives of our premies and alleviate their pain, others assist in the voluntary killing and disposal of identical babies.

Actual experiences of several people were combined to create the characters in this story. We allow them to tell us the truth about the painful experiences of losing a baby, but also the lasting effects of loss, no matter the cause or circumstance. They show us how to find hope behind our veil of tears.

# A Chance Meeting

The uncontrollable tears were driving Monica nuts. She pushed down her emotions as she walked. Her daily trips to the mall were part of her therapy for getting over the trauma. Her people-watching skills had become very acute, and she enjoyed the spectacle that took place around her.

Just ahead, she spotted a toddler being dragged down the corridor. He was screaming and refused to go where his mom was leading. Apparently, the toy store two storefronts back was still holding his attention. As the scene drew attention from all the onlookers, the mom picked him up and, with one motion, tucked him under her arm. He continued kicking his feet and flailing his arms off to her side. Her only comment: "You are coming with me, young man, whether you like it or not. When you start behaving, I will let you down, but not until then." This apparently struck a chord in the toddler's brain because he immediately went limp and quiet. Something told Monica that he would have been wedged under his mother's strong arm for a long time if he hadn't changed his behavior.

Monica smiled and kept walking. Up ahead a young mom sat on a wooden bench at the edge of the concourse. She looked tired. She had a stroller sitting beside her, and she glanced down once in a while to check on her baby. Apparently, she too liked to watch the spectacle at the mall. When she wasn't checking on her baby, she studied the passersby. Monica's eyes met hers, and they seemed to connect. Instead of glancing away, as she usually did if someone returned her stare, Monica held this mother in her gaze. Then she slowly walked over to the woman and greeted her as she approached.

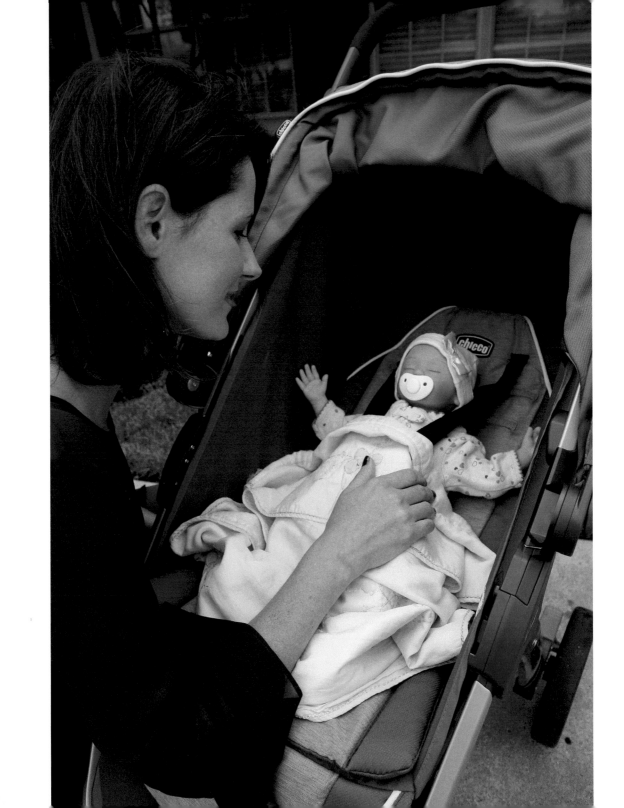

The woman introduced herself as Julie. "And this is little Miss Allison. We call her Allie." Monica peered into the stroller to look at Miss Allison. Instead of the baby she expected to see, she saw a doll. The doll's eyes were closed, and she was covered with a thin blanket. Monica thought, *This woman is crazy, pushing a doll around in a stroller, passing it off as a real baby.* She was just about ready to turn and walk away when baby Allison moved her arm and audibly sighed.

Monica gasped, and Julie caught her confused expression. "Yes, she's real." Julie smiled as Monica took in all of Allison's tiny features. "She was born five months ago, but she's really only two weeks old."

"Wait a minute. How can that be?" asked Monica with a puzzled look on her face. She tried to do the math in her head but couldn't remember exactly how many weeks a regular pregnancy lasts.

"Well," replied Julie, "Allie was born seventeen weeks early because I went into preterm labor."

"Wow, that is amazing. I have never seen a baby this small." The truth was that Monica had seen a baby that small, but the thought of it was so painful that she was trying to erase it from her memory.

"Allie is my miracle baby," said Julie proudly. She went on to describe her baby's struggle for survival. Monica listened intently. "Her gestational age was just under twenty-three weeks when she was delivered," Julie explained. Monica's demeanor visibly changed as her expression became somber.

"She was so fragile back then. She was in so much pain," Julie concluded.

Monica, now visibly agitated, interjected, "No, that is not possible. I've been told babies that young don't feel any pain. How do *you* know your baby felt pain at twenty-three weeks?"

"I know because I watched her have surgery."

# Julie

The respirator beat out a monotone rhythm, interrupted only by the occasional bells and alarms from all the monitors. Little Allison lay motionless in her incubator. Her mother knew that something was wrong but couldn't quite put her finger on it. Allie just wasn't acting right. She usually was a feisty little thing, with her fiery red hair matching her personality. This morning, however, she seemed like a limp rag.

The nurse finished checking Billy, the baby next to Allie. He was a strapping young boy, weighing four times that of Miss Allie. He was only eight weeks premature compared with Allie's almost eighteen weeks. Billy was breathing on his own and was even sporadically tolerating bottle feeds. Allie, on the other hand, depended almost entirely on her intravenous feeds to survive.

Many times, Julie had stared longingly at Billy. He was so healthy, so beautiful. One time, she watched as Billy's mom gave him a bath. She lovingly scrubbed him clean, kissing his little feet as she worked. She even combed his fine, straight hair when she was finished. Julie had never been able to kiss Allie. She didn't even have enough hair to comb. Now Billy was nestled against his mother's chest, placed there by his nurse. He fell asleep almost instantly as his mother rocked and comforted him.

Allie was trapped in her plastic prison. Julie's only occasional contact with her was to press her face against the wall of the incubator as she reached in to touch the baby's delicate, almost transparent, hands and fingers. Julie dreamed of just once holding Allie in her arms, quieting her tiny cries.

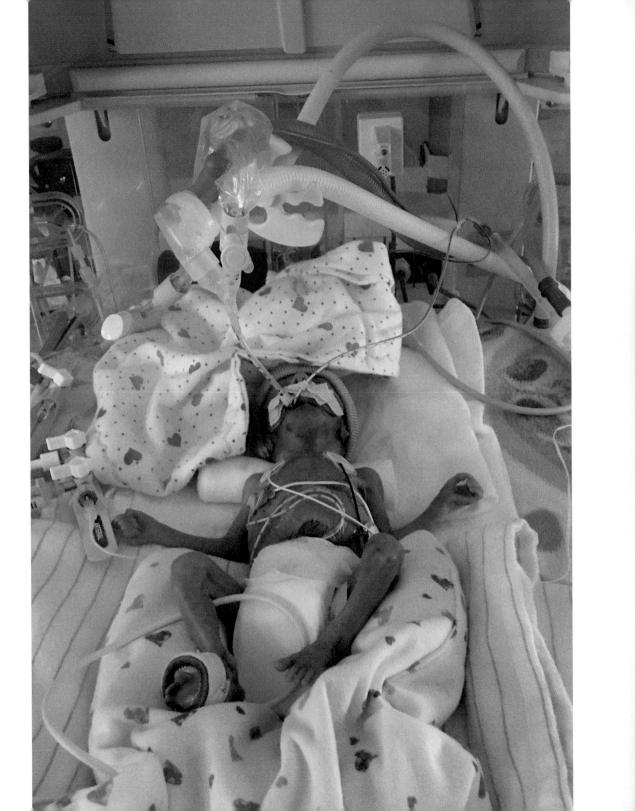

Julie thought back on her pregnancy. She had been jubilant when she discovered she was pregnant. She and her husband, Bill, had been trying for years to conceive. They were sitting in their fertility specialist's office waiting for the results of the latest blood work when they got the good news.

They had sat in these seats before, after their second round of in-vitro fertilization. That visit ended in deep disappointment when Julie's fertility doctor told her that she had a hostile uterus, which rejected the fertilized eggs. This later became the source of a running joke between Bill and Julie, blaming her "hostile uterus" for causing any problem that came up. Bill would say, "It must be that hostile uterus of yours."

On their way home after that fateful visit, Julie sat quietly crying in the passenger seat. Bill knew this from her quietness and the tears trickling down her cheeks. He broke the silence, "Don't despair, Jules. Things will work out. We only need to keep moving ahead believing God will provide us with a child to raise. I do have an idea, something I have been thinking about for a while. How about adopting a baby?"

"What kind of baby?"

"Is there more than one kind of baby?"

"Of course! Our friends, Tim and Donna, adopted a baby girl from China."

"Do you want a girl from China?"

"No, not necessarily. I would be happy with any baby, but maybe we could talk to their adoption agency."

"I agree that we could adopt any kind of baby, but I'm thinking of getting one from a little closer to home than China."

"That would be awesome."

"Do you remember George Williams, my roommate from college?"

"Yeah, but you haven't seen him in years."

"Well that's not strictly true. We video conferenced last week. It seems that, after law school, he specialized in adoption law. He has many contacts, and he referred me to the finest agency he knows."

"Why did you do that?"

"I wanted a backup plan in case we didn't get pregnant."

On their way home, they considered the possibilities adoption afforded them. Julie stopped crying. Bill smiled.

They began investigating the adoption process together. Ironically, failing to get pregnant brought Julie and Bill closer together. The idea of adoption brought closure to the failed artificial conception techniques. Julie found solace in the thought of their adopted baby, even though they were not even close to holding an actual baby in their arms.

Julie was relieved to be done with all the ultrasounds, and the invasive procedures, and the drugs that messed with her hormone balance. It was in the midst of all the adoption paperwork and interviews that Julie noticed the changes in her body that led her and Bill back into those seats at the fertility clinic.

Julie had never been happier. She and Bill had worked so hard to have a baby, and now it had just happened without any planning or preparation. The pregnancy felt like a miracle. Julie and Bill went to work immediately to create a nursery, including many trips to various stores to pick out furniture and other elements of décor. They worked at night and on weekends, cleaning, painting, and decorating. Julie remembered these days with great fondness. The nursery was adorable, filled with lambs and bunnies.

Julie's best friend, Janet, decided to throw a baby shower for her. After several conversations about the shower on the phone, the two women decided to meet over lunch. Midway through Janet's list of possible funny party games, including the one in which diapers are filled with simulated poo made out of melted candy bars, Julie felt a pain in her back and sides. She must have grimaced because Janet asked her, "Julie, are you all right? You look a little pale."

"I'm fine, I think Bill and I overdid it last night assembling the new crib."

Janet saw through Julie's flimsy explanation. She had delivered several children herself and recognized the onset of labor pains. Of course, Julie rubbing her sides made it pretty obvious. She said to her friend, "I don't think so, Julie. How long has this been going on?"

"It started on my way over here. Kind of a back-spasm thing."

"I think you're starting labor.'

"That can't be! I am not due for another four months."

"You had better call your doctor."

That phone call landed her in the emergency room. From there she was transferred to labor and delivery with a monitor strapped to her stomach. Julie called Bill, and he rushed to her side. "We're starting you on medication to stop the labor," explained her obstetrician. "We're also giving you steroids to mature your baby's lungs. If you respond promptly to treatment, you might be able to go home for a while on strict bed rest."

Julie was distraught. "Am I going to lose my baby?" she asked as she dug her nails into Bill's arm.

"Not necessarily. If it were born today, then, yes, you would lose your baby. However, if we can stop your labor and mature its lungs enough, we have a chance for viability."

"Does viability mean survival?" asked Bill tentatively.

"In the short term, I would say yes. In the long term, I cannot say because so much can happen to a premature infant. Here is what I can tell you: the longer your baby stays inside your womb, the better. Every day we can keep your baby inside, the better the odds become for survival outside, both in the short and long term."

Julie did respond to treatment, and she went home for a few days. Her hope buoyed. Each day she replayed her obstetrician's words in her mind: "Every day we can keep your baby inside, the better the odds become for survival." Each day she prayed, *One more day, God. Let me keep my baby just one more day.* Allison's birth came at just the right time. Her lungs had matured enough to tolerate the ventilator and provide oxygen to her tissues.

Dr. Jen Proust, the neonatologist caring for little Allie in the neonatal intensive care unit (NICU) came to Julie's room in the labor and delivery unit to give her an update. "Your baby was born extremely premature. She is very fragile right now. Her skin is paper thin and translucent. You will be able to see all her arteries and veins right through her skin. All the rest of her organs are also fragile. Her brain, eyes, and even her intestines are at risk. She is prone to infections in her lungs, IV sites, and her bloodstream. We have started antibiotics already and have done blood cultures. We have placed a tube in her windpipe, and she is on a breathing machine. We gave her surfactant to make it easier for her to breathe. We inserted special IV lines into her umbilical vein and one of her umbilical arteries."

Julie responded, "Whoa, doctor, that is a lot to process. Could you give that to me in more simple terms?"

"I understand. Most people want lots of detail. Here's the take-home version: Your baby is fragile and vulnerable to many possible complications of prematurity. We have taken over several of her body's normal functions such as breathing and eating."

"Is Allie going to die?" asked Julie.

"At this point she has about a fifty-fifty chance for survival. Each week that passes improves those odds."

"Is there anything I can do to help her? I feel so helpless."

"It's well known that human interaction is helpful in the development of all babies, premies included. She knows your voice from the womb. When you open the door of the incubator, talk to her. Let her know you are there. When she is older you can hold her on your chest. We call it kangaroo care."

Julie's first encounter with Allie was terrifying and wondrous all at the same time. Tubes, wires, and probes seemed to be inserted or attached to almost every part of her body. Julie understood very quickly Dr. Proust's warnings about how fragile Allie would be. She faithfully spoke to Miss Allie every time she was around the incubator, whether the doors were open or closed. She knew in the back of her mind that sometimes this was more for her benefit than Allie's. She felt the bond created in the womb strengthening each time she touched the translucent fingers or stroked the fuzz on Allie's head.

One time, Julie was devastated because Allie needed a blood transfusion, and the nurse had to start a new IV. The thought of needles repeatedly jabbing Allie's skin was horrifying. Another time, Julie was exhilarated because Dr. Proust allowed Allie to get feeds through her nasogastric tube. She called them "gut-stimulating feeds" or "priming feeds" and explained that they would help with the growth and development of her intestines. Julie pumped breast milk constantly to provide for these feeds. Providing food was another tangible thing she could do help her baby.

Julie's hopes had been soaring since Dr Proust removed Allie's umbilical lines. She had replaced them with a peripherally inserted central catheter line (PICC). For Julie, a sense of a future for her and her baby was forming and beginning to take hold. All this was in jeopardy because of what Julie suspected was now happening. A sick feeling was taking hold of her.

The nurse came over to Allie's incubator and began her routine check of the pumps, intravenous solutions, incubator temperature, and myriad other seemingly insignificant details.

"I think Allie is sick. Could you please check her out?" Julie implored, wiping a tear from her moist eyes. "She hasn't been moving much for the last hour or so. Something's not right."

"Well, let's take a look," responded Laura Fields, Allie's nurse.

Julie really liked Laura. She was an experienced NICU nurse. Julie imagined that there were very few situations Laura could not handle. This is why she was holding herself together, barely. She thought, *Laura will know what to do.*

"Allie has been doing very well lately, and I'm scared something really bad is happening," Julie stammered between her sobs.

Laura slipped an understanding arm around Julie's shoulders and gave her a sideways hug. "We never give up hope here in the NICU. Let's see what Allie's doing."

She immediately turned on the exam light and opened the two small doors in the side of the incubator. She opened Allie's tiny diaper and gasped at what she saw. Laura motioned for Julie to come over and look. Both peered into the incubator and saw a most disturbing sight. Allie's normally small belly was bloated and had a horrible blue-green hue. The diaper contained a seedy yellow stool, which Julie was used to seeing, but there was blood mixed in with the poo.

"What's wrong with her belly?" Julie asked, "and what's with the blood in the poo?"

"I'm not sure, but we'll have the neonatologist come look at her."

The next few minutes were a blur of activity. Julie watched as Dr. Proust examined Allie. She obviously was very concerned about her big green belly. Her expression was stern as she listened with her stethoscope. She stood motionless listening for the bowel sounds that normally graced her ears. They were absent. She pushed on Allie's normally squishy belly but found instead a hard, rigid, and tender belly. She looked at the monitors that indicated a racing heart, falling blood pressure, and increasing need for oxygen.

Dr. Proust, taking all of this in, snapped into action. She barked out instructions for the nurses ordering blood tests, X-rays, antibiotic infusions, and a surgical consultation. She walked over to Julie, now seated in a chair just outside Allie's room. Dr. Proust's expression was still grave, but she did soften as she approached. She slid off her exam gloves and filled her palms with sterilizing foam. She forced a smile as she unconsciously massaged the foam onto her hands and arms. She was just ready to talk to Julie, but a phone call halted her advance. She took the call just outside of Julie's hearing. It was the surgeon whom Dr. Proust had called to discuss Allie's case.

Dr. Proust was still talking on the phone when the portable X-ray machine rumbled down the corridor. The technician arrived and slid an X-ray plate under Allie and snapped a picture. She then stood the plate up beside her belly and snapped a second picture. The technician motioned to Dr. Proust to come view the films. She studied the images and then muttered in a barely audible voice, "Just as I thought."

Laura brought a paper printout from the rapid blood testing done on a machine in the NICU. She showed it to Dr. Proust. The pair walked over to Julie, who had been closely watching all the activity from her nearby seat.

"Julie," began Dr. Proust, "You are right. There is something wrong with Allie." Her voice was comforting as was her demeanor. Julie knew Dr. Proust loved her neonates almost as much as the mothers did. She was very protective. The doctor's words, however, brought little comfort: "We think Allison has an infection of her intestines."

"You mean like the flu?" Julie asked, interrupting Dr. Proust.

"No, this is much more serious. This infection can cause the intestines to die. It sometimes moves very quickly. We caught the infection early, but it appears there is already a perforation or hole in the gut."

"Will she be all right?"

"We hope so. I have started several powerful antibiotics to try to stop the infection. Dr. George Newberry has been called to come see your baby. He is our pediatric surgeon. He will tell us the next step in her treatment. I will defer to him for any further discussion of the treatment options."

Julie was a mess as she waited for the surgeon to arrive. She called her husband, Bill, and filled him in on all the developments. He was out of town with his job, but agreed to come home immediately.

Doctor Newberry came quickly to the NICU. He was dressed in scrubs and wore a brightly colored scrub hat with cartoon characters on it. His patients loved the many different hats he wore. As he arrived, the nurses warmly greeted him. He was all business, though, and politely responded to them, not stopping to chat.

He came straight to Allie's room and greeted Julie as he washed his hands in the sink just inside the sliding door. He introduced himself, "Hello, I'm Dr. Newberry. I'm the pediatric surgeon. Dr. Proust called me to see your little girl." He glanced up at the name card on the side of the incubator and continued, "Allison." He opened the doors and carefully examined Miss Allie. Julie quietly slipped back into Allie's room and watched him work.

Laura came in and said, "Dr. Newberry, let me pop the top. This is one of those fancy beds. We can convert it at the touch of a button to provide heat from above." She pushed the button with the up arrow on it, and sure enough the top of the incubator rose into the air and immediately began radiating heat to keep Allie warm. Laura and Dr. Newberry dropped the plastic sides of the incubator, giving Julie her first unobstructed view of her baby girl.

Allie's belly seemed to expand as he examined her. Each time Dr. Newberry pushed on Allie's tiny abdomen, she grimaced and silently cried. She arched her back and tried to get away from the hand causing the pain. As he was conducting his examination, Dr. Newberry explained to Julie, "Allie has succumbed to a disease that strikes only premies. It is called necrotizing enterocolitis. It's eating away at her gut. It has already caused a section of bowel to die and fall apart. Bowel contents have spilled into her belly, causing the dark green discoloration that you can see very plainly. Allie is too sick to undergo surgery to remove the dead gut, so we will perform a temporary surgery right here in the NICU."

Julie was now standing next to Dr. Newberry staring at her precious little girl teetering on the brink of death. She was panicked and looked over helplessly at the only physician who had the expertise to save her baby. She saw confidence and hope. Doctor Newberry looked back at Julie, and he saw frustration and despair. He was not surprised when she broke down and buried her head in his shoulder. Her body heaved as she sobbed uncontrollably. He did not rebuke or reject her. He seemed totally confident handling the whole situation. His actions were smooth and natural. He gently slipped his arm around her and gave a comforting hug.

"Can she survive the anesthetic?" Julie asked between sobs.

"Allison's body cannot tolerate a full anesthetic because of the toxins and acid building up in her blood. We will instead give her a narcotic called fentanyl through her IV. After that, we'll use some lidocaine—a local anesthetic—to block the pain in the skin. Even with all that, she will feel pain when we go through the lining of the abdominal cavity. The peritoneum is very difficult to block. We'll do our best to make her comfortable while still being safe."

Julie heard his words, but they didn't seem real. She did not want to face this horrifying reality, so her mind took her somewhere else. She escaped into a happier place free from pain. Her mind was reeling as Laura guided her to the sofa in the back of Allie's room. Doctor Newberry immediately went to work setting up his sterile table of instruments and supplies. Laura sat with Julie quietly going over what Dr. Newberry had said. She made sure Julie understood everything that was going to happen. Julie consented to the surgery and was allowed to watch from her seat on the sofa as Dr. Newberry began the procedure. He was being assisted by a surgery resident. Julie thought the resident was way too young to be a doctor, but she could tell that Dr. Newberry trusted him and wanted him to succeed by how he treated him.

The resident washed Allie's belly with some iodine soap and laid sterile towels around the surgical site. The nurse pushed drugs through the IV as Dr. Newberry injected the local anesthetic. Allie lurched with the needle stick. Julie clenched her fists and bit her lip. She wanted them to stop the procedure. Dr. Newberry continued with a scalpel and hemostat clamp. He broke into the abdominal cavity just as he had described. Julie heard an audible "pop." Allie squirmed. No one heard her painful scream except Julie, and that only in her mind.

A fountain of green and black fluid resembling motor oil gushed out of the tense abdomen. Dr. Newberry washed the cavity out with saline solution and then threaded a rubber drain into the belly.

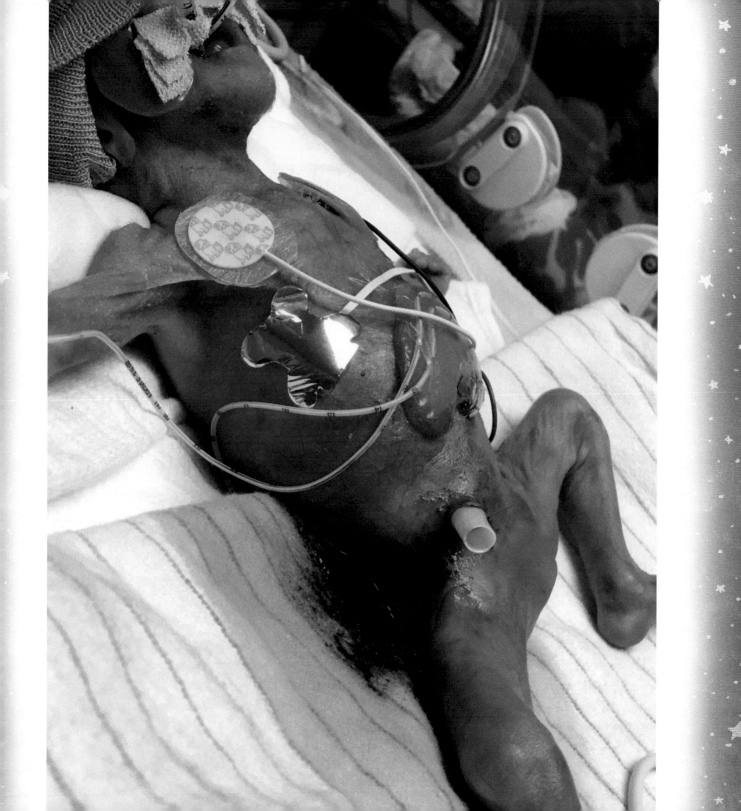

The green drainage kept coming out even after gauze was piled high on the wound.

As Dr. Newberry finished, he gave orders for the nurse to carry out. He told her, "Change the dressing as needed. I expect a large amount of drainage. You can even put a stoma bag over the site if necessary. Also, put her on a fentanyl drip, two micrograms per kilo per hour. She's going to need a lot of narcotics."

Dr. Newberry turned and spoke to Julie, who was still seated on the couch. Her composure had returned, and she eagerly listened to his words. "Allison is critically ill. If the drain we placed works, then she may have a chance at survival. I am not sure she has the strength to pull through. We'll see what happens overnight. If she turns the corner, then in several days or so we will do the big surgery. In the meantime, we will do everything in our power to save her. I'm putting her on a narcotic drip to keep her comfortable. She's in a lot of pain from the stool that has leaked into her belly."

Dr. Newberry turned to the resident and asked if he had any questions. The two discussed Allie's medical condition and the procedure. Julie did not understand all the medical jargon until the end of their conversation when she overheard Dr. Newberry saying, "It's hard to believe that ten years ago some physicians didn't believe that premies felt any pain. They thought that their pain receptors weren't developed yet. Pain is actually felt very early by the developing fetus. Allison was born at twenty-three weeks gestational age. Twenty years ago, she would have died because we didn't have the high-tech ventilators that we do now or surfactant. Our understanding of the fetus continues to grow as younger and younger babies are being saved. It seems that these second-trimester babies are much like their older counterparts when it comes to pain. They have very well developed pain sensation. Ask Laura. She'll tell you all about it."

Laura nodded her head in agreement and replied quietly. "Yeah, it's tough when we have to start difficult IVs. The babies scream and fuss each time we stick them. Their heart rate and respiratory rates go up and set off their alarms."

The resident nodded thoughtfully and looked down at Allison. He had never seen a baby this small, but hoped that the surgery would give her a chance at survival. He turned to Dr. Newberry, asking about their next patient, and they took their leave. As Laura began to clean up the operation site, Julie looked up at her and asked "D—did they really mean all that?"

Laura sighed. "Sorry. They can be kind of blunt sometimes. Yes, Allie feels pain, but we wouldn't do anything more than necessary for her health. I promise we're doing all we can."

Allie survived the surgery, and Julie refused to leave her side. Many dressing changes were necessary. Each pile of gauze, however, had less and less green stuff on it. Dr. Newberry came back the next day and washed Allie's belly out again with warm saline. Bill had returned in the wee hours of the morning and stood by Julie's side watching the procedure. "I think Allie is improving!" said Dr. Newberry with a note of optimism. "The drainage is slowing down, but I still think there is a hole in the gut." As Dr. Newberry finished this sentence, as if on cue, Allie pulled up her legs, and air bubbled out of her wound.

"Is she ready for surgery yet?" asked Julie as she clutched Bill's hand.

"Let's give it another day or two. Her platelets are coming up, and her CRP is coming down."

Bill chirped in, "Platelets, CRP—what are those?"

"Platelets are responsible for blood clotting. They drop when babies get necrotizing enterocolitis. It is a good sign when they come back up. Hopefully the necrotizing process has stopped and we can go in to remove the damaged bowel. CRP means C-reactive protein. It's a protein produced in the liver, and the level jumps with any infection or inflammation. It is a general guide to improvement or deterioration. It's good that Allie's level is going down."

"That's encouraging," responded Julie with a smile on her face.

Julie's smile grew over the next two days. Allie was given some blood, and her color looked so much better. The bruising on her abdomen was fading, and she looked pink again. Dr. Newberry had announced the day before that she was ready for surgery and scheduled it for today. This surgery was to be performed under anesthesia but still in the NICU. A whole host of people had paraded through Allie's room. The anesthesiologist discussed putting her to sleep. Dr. Newberry discussed the surgery. The operating room nurse asked Julie a series of questions and then had her sign the consent forms. Surgery technicians brought carts of supplies and instruments to the corridor outside Allie's room. Bill and Julie were then ushered out of Allie's room and taken to the NICU family lounge.

When Dr. Newberry arrived in the lounge after the surgery, he found the parents sitting together on a couch in the corner. Julie was resting her head on Bill's chest. Dr. Newberry was obviously happy about something because his eyes were beaming and he was almost grinning. He was accompanied by Dr. Proust. "Allie is doing great," Dr. Newberry said. "She tolerated the surgery well, and we had no problems. We removed part of her small bowel but preserved all of her colon. We brought out one end of the bowel as a stoma. She will poop into a small bag. The other end is tied off but still is connected to the anus."

"That's disgusting," said Julie with a frown on her face.

"You won't think so after you get used to it," responded Dr. Newberry.

"What are her chances for survival now?" asked Bill.

"I think they are good. We can ask Dr. Proust what she thinks."

He looked over at her and she responded, "I agree. It is amazing she has made it this far and under this much stress without bleeding into her brain, but her head ultrasound yesterday was normal. Her lungs are in good shape. She has lost very little bowel. She has a good shot of coming through all this undamaged."

"We have a long road ahead of us," cautioned Dr. Newberry. "There will be another surgery to put her back together."

"When will that happen?" asked Julie.

"Probably about six weeks from now," he answered

"Can we see her yet?" Bill enquired.

"Yes," responded Dr. Proust, "but don't expect much from her. She is still coming out of the anesthesia. We have increased her pain medications, so she might be sleepy."

Every day Julie saw improvement in Allie's condition. Feedings were restarted after two weeks. Her antibiotics were stopped at the same time. The process of healing seemed slow and painful, yet hopeful and bright. Dr. Proust slowly increased the amount of food she received. Feeding her baby with a tube and a syringe reminded Julie of the techniques used by people who rescued baby animals. The amount of milk Allie was getting at each feeding was just a fraction of an ounce and would have fit in one of those eyedroppers they used.

Allie took all her feeds via her nasogastric feeding tube. She lived in her incubator because she still could not keep her body temperature high enough without it. Julie helped out with Allie's care as much as possible. She changed her diapers when she was with her. The diapers were so small. They were like diapers for a toy doll.

By the time Dr. Newberry closed Allie's stoma, she was tolerating full feeds via her feeding tube. She was gaining weight very well. Her head ultrasounds all came back normal. Her eye exams all were normal and showed no signs of retinal disease caused by prematurity. Her lungs were improving, and she was weaned off the ventilator to high-flow nasal cannula oxygen. Dr. Proust told Julie that it was almost unheard of for a baby as premature as Allie to escape without any long-term effects. So far they had found none.

After Allie's stoma closure, she started pooping into her diaper. Julie was so happy to change Allie's soiled diapers. Just as Dr. Newberry predicted, the baby's weight gain accelerated when the rest of the gut was put back into circulation. Another milestone was getting out of the incubator. Julie was allowed to do "kangaroo care"—placing Allie on her bare chest. She would sit and talk to Allie as she rocked. She would sometimes sing to her. This was a time of intense bonding. Julie would later look back at this time as her favorite part of Allie's time in the neonatal unit.

Bill noticed that Julie would absolutely glow with happiness every time she returned home from her visits with Allie. Three months after Allie's first surgery, she was tolerating bottle feedings. She had more than tripled her birth weight and looked fat.

The night before Allie's discharge home from the hospital, Julie sat rocking her. She was trying to get Allie to settle down.

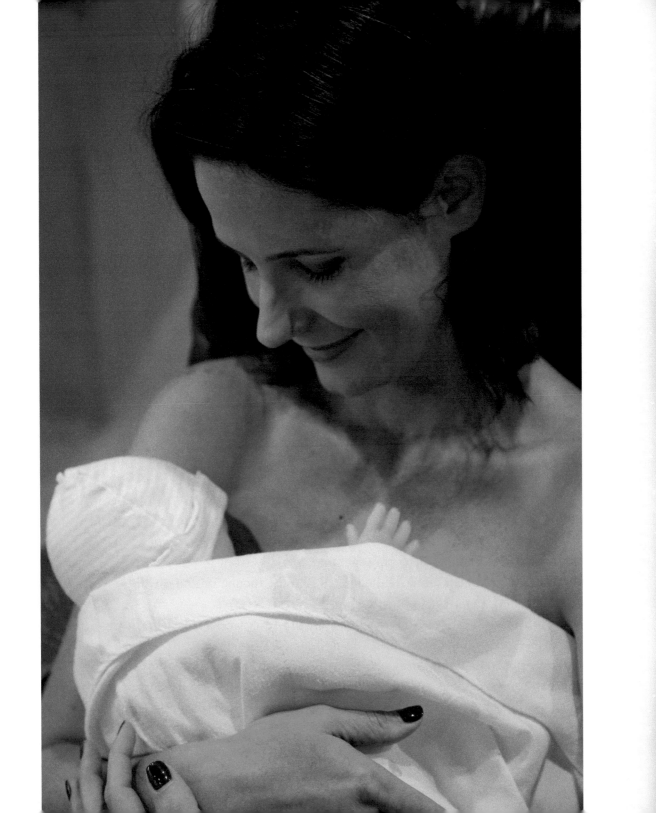

Allie was fussing because she'd just had her diaper changed and was getting hungry. Julie rocked and spoke gently to little Allie, comforting her into silence. Allie fell asleep snuggled up against Julie's warm chest. The past three months flashed across Julie's memory—all the ups and downs. She recalled her dread at almost losing Allie, but also remembered the exhilaration of the day that she fed Allie her first bottle.

As Julie sat reminiscing, she looked across the hallway to a young mother who was peering longingly into an incubator. Inside was another precious little life being kept alive by intravenous drips and machines. A flood of emotion washed over Julie. Her heart leapt out to the worried mom across the room. Empathetic tears streamed down her cheeks as she thought about her own baby's miraculous progress and what the other mother was experiencing.

How jealous Julie had been of Billy's mother. Now she was the mom holding her baby. She rocked silently back and forth and breathed a prayer.

Julie thanked God that Allie had been protected against all the complications of prematurity. She was grateful for her baby's miraculous healing through the knowledge and skills of Dr. Newberry and Dr. Proust. She asked God to help her be a good mom and to raise Allie to fulfill her special purpose. Julie was convinced that God had an amazing plan for Allie's life. This thought alone caused her heart to swell with love and hope.

It was in the midst of this happiness that Julie felt so drawn to the mom she barely knew. She wanted to give her just a glimpse of hope to help her through this difficult part. Julie prayed just audibly, "Please, God, help that baby across the room. Keep her safe just like you did Allie. Comfort her mom as you did me."

Julie looked up at the young mother, who was no longer peering into the incubator. She was staring at Julie and Allie, just as Julie had stared at Billy and his mom. Julie knew exactly what she must do. She slipped Allie into her bassinet and walked over to the woman. "How old is your baby?"

"She's about a week old. My placenta separated partially from my uterus causing early labor when I was only twenty-eight weeks along." Julie looked into the incubator and saw little Adele hooked up to tubes just as Allie had been.

"My little Allison—we call her Allie—was only twenty-three weeks old when she was born. I remember when she was all tubes and wires just like Adele."

"How did you handle all the worry and stress?"

"My husband and family helped support me. Dr. Proust was a big help too, but truthfully it was and is my faith in God that got me through. In fact, as I was rocking Allie I saw you across the unit and I said a prayer for you."

"That is really sweet of you. Thank you."

"Are you married?"

"My husband is a long-haul truck driver. He comes and visits when he is in town, but that isn't very often."

"My Bill is a regional manager for a drug store chain. He is gone a lot too. Would you like to meet at a restaurant sometime for lunch?"

"Okay. I would enjoy that."

The two women hugged as only mothers of sick neonates can. This was the start of a relationship that would endure beyond the neonatal intensive care unit.

Allie was still tiny when she went home from the hospital. She left the unit before her due date, weighing just over four pounds. Julie had seen other babies go home with feeding tubes in their noses, but not Allie. Other premies needed oxygen at home because of their chronic lung disease, but not Allie. She did require a continuous apnea monitor. She had no bleeding in her brain or damage to her retinas as other premies had. Doctor Proust told Julie many times that Allie was a miracle baby. She appeared to have no permanent damage from being born premature.

Julie's family threw a party on the day Allie came home. There was nothing but joy and celebration surrounding her baby. This was how Julie saw the world—a happy, miraculous place. She knew from her time in the NICU, however, that there were many families that saw the world differently. She knew even the mention of a premature baby threw some parents into a new cycle of grief and sorrow.

# Monica

Monica's reaction to Allie's ordeal didn't surprise or upset Julie. She assumed Monica had suffered a tragedy involving a baby. The pain was obviously fresh and raw, and her emotions were still out of control.

The onlookers in the mall were becoming visibly agitated with Monica's public display of intense emotion. Julie quickly suggested they have a meal together in a nearby restaurant. Monica nodded her assent, and they retired to a quiet area in the back of the restaurant. Julie knew several of the waitresses there from her frequent trips with Allison. The waitress who seated them was very respectful of the two women.

Julie decided not to press Monica for information or explanation. She sat quietly, keeping her eye on Allie who amazingly remained asleep in the stroller, which was now parked beside the booth. At first Monica could not even look at the menu, let alone at Julie, but just sat there, face down and shoulders heaving.

Monica had always been athletic. She played basketball, ran track and cross-country in high school. She played basketball on a full-ride scholarship at the state university. She graduated with a degree in marketing and took a job with a national apparel company. She still ran two to three times each week, weather permitting. She worked out frequently and was proud of her perfect physique. It was at the gym that she met Robert, who was very muscular. He came frequently to lift weights. They exchanged glances at first, and then engaged in sporadic conversation. They found they had a lot of common interests. Robert had also played basketball in college.

Robert and Monica frequently communicated but never committed to a relationship. That changed one day when Robert saw Monica struggling on a stair climber. He went over to her. "You look sweaty today."

"Thanks for the compliment," she retorted sarcastically. "Get your butt on one of these and see how dry you stay."

He immediately jumped on the climber next to her and began an aggressive workout. "I was hoping to see you today."

"Oh, why is that?" she queried.

"My office is having an employee appreciation dinner this weekend."

"So, how does that affect me?" she asked coyly.

"Well," stammered Robert, "I was hoping you could come with me."

"Are you asking me on a date?"

"Uh, yes, I am."

"I would be pleased to come with you."

Monica's world changed that day. She went to the party with Robert and met several of his friends from the office. They were all great guys who hassled and mocked Robert constantly. She could see that they were all good friends. She was surprised at how well she fit into their world. She and Robert fell madly in love. They dated for several months and found happiness together.

Most of their dates were at clubs where they went dancing and drinking. They did go to some local concerts. One evening they were sitting together at new popular restaurant. "I have been thinking about us," Robert began.

"Yes, what exactly have you been pondering?" asked Monica. She was worried this could be a break-up speech.

"We've been spending a lot of time together lately."

"Yes we have. That's a good thing, right?"

"It's a very good thing. I find myself wanting to spend more time with you."

Now Monica thought this could be a proposal instead. She eagerly replied, "And I want to spend all my time with you."

"So let's go find a condo or house we can lease together and get rid of our apartments."

"Okay," she replied with a slight tinge of disappointment. "That could work. We would definitely see more of each other."

"Let's start looking tomorrow."

Robert ordered champagne to celebrate. He toasted to their future together: "Monica, I love you, and want to spend my life with you. Here's to our future."

Monica and Robert spent a week looking for a condo. They found the perfect location at the right price. Robert treated her with such respect and kindness. He was always the gentleman. Their next five months were like a fairy tale. Everyone who knew them called them "the perfect couple." They fit so well together. But getting pregnant was not part of their plans. When Monica discovered she was having a baby, she was happy about it. She looked forward to their future as a family. She hoped now Robert would finally ask her to marry him.

She made a special dinner for Robert and planned to tell him that she was pregnant during the course of the meal. "Robert," she began as she was about to serve dessert, "I have some wonderful news."

"Did you get a promotion at work?"

"No, something better. I am pregnant!" She expected a smile and congratulations, but got only silence. Her heart dropped like a rock falling off a cliff. In fact, she felt as if she had just been shoved off the cliff. "Aren't you happy?" she asked with moistening eyes.

Robert stumbled, "Uh, yeah I don't know what to say."

"How about, 'I'm so happy for you' or 'That's wonderful'?"

"This is not what we planned."

"Well, planned or not, *this* did happen."

Robert mumbled, "I'm sorry. I'm not hungry. I have to go think about this." He got up, grabbed his coat and keys, and rushed out of the house. Tears slid down Monica's cheeks. She sat and sobbed.

She had no idea where Robert had gone until she got a call from one of his buddies. Robert had drunk himself into a stupor, and they were bringing him home. One of his other friends drove his car home for him. Monica thanked them as they deposited an unconscious Robert on the couch.

The next day he felt terrible about his actions and presented Monica with roses and an apology. "Look, I'm sorry about last night. I freaked out. I'm not ready to be a dad. Give me some time to adjust to the idea."

"I accept your apology, Robert. What can I do to help you?"

"Nothing. I am scared to death of having a baby. I'm just not ready."

"We have nine months to figure this out."

"Let's put this behind us for now. We'll talk later."

Unfortunately, later never came, and Robert did not deal with his fear. He started going out without Monica to be with his "buddies." He started drinking more and more. He often came home drunk. Monica's concern for Robert's drinking grew. She confronted him, "Robert we need to talk."

"Talk about what?"

"About the baby growing inside my belly." She pointed to her abdomen; barely a bump was visible.

"Not this again."

"You owe it to yourself and your future child to figure it out."

"Figure what out?"

"Figure out that you are not spending any time with me anymore. Figure out that you are drinking too much."

"I don't drink too much. And besides, what's wrong with spending time with my friends? They don't judge me like you do."

"I'm not judging you. I'm stating facts. If you don't stop drinking so much, you will become an alcoholic."

"You know this is all your fault."

"How is that possible?"

"Everything was fine before you got pregnant. If you would just get rid of the baby …"

Monica bristled at this suggestion. She wanted the baby. This situation was not the baby's fault. The fault was Robert's unnatural fear of becoming a father. This was just one of many fights. The arguing escalated when Robert started bringing bottles of hard liquor home. He drank himself senseless many nights.

Robert blamed his drinking on her pregnancy. She eventually accepted this because before the pregnancy he had drunk very little, and now he was on the verge of becoming an alcoholic. Monica was constantly looking for a way to change Robert's attitude and behavior.

Monica's initial excitement about having the baby faded over time. The baby was tearing her and Robert apart. It was driving him to excessive drinking. Monica began to blame all her troubles on the baby and wished that she had never gotten pregnant. More and more she came to hate the whole situation. Why had she ever agreed to move in with Robert?

Robert became moody and more prone to angry outbursts. Monica felt their relationship unraveling. He finally packed up his stuff one day while Monica was at work and moved out. When Monica arrived home that night she found all Robert's clothing and belongings gone. The only thing he had left behind was a half-empty bottle of whiskey. Monica felt a mix of emotions. On the one hand, she was devastated that the father of her child had walked out on them, but on the other hand, she was relieved that the fighting would be over. Mostly she felt empty and incomplete.

Monica was at the point of desperation when she saw an ad for a local abortion clinic. She wanted to call the number, but was troubled by the thought of losing her baby. It took a few days, but her desire to reconcile with Robert won out in the end. She called the number and made an appointment for the next morning. She had called her own obstetrician first, but found out she did not perform abortions. Monica talked to Robert that night on the phone and told him about her plan. He seemed pleased that she had made the appointment and agreed to pay all her expenses for the abortion. She thought he seemed more like himself again. She remembered all the happy times she and Robert had spent together before she got pregnant. She recalled all the fights they'd had after she got pregnant. It made sense that their relationship might be put back together again if she could just get rid of her baby. Her happiness would then be restored.

Monica drove to her nine o'clock appointment at the clinic. Her best friend from work, Danni, accompanied her. She and Monica had spent many hours discussing her situation, and Danni agreed this would be the best choice for Monica. "Are you absolutely sure this is the best choice?" asked Monica as she drove.

Danni then posed a series of questions to Monica: "What if you actually have the baby? What then? Robert doesn't want to be a father. So, do you want to raise the baby as a single parent? What kind of life will that be? This will be so much better. Much simpler."

"Maybe Robert will come around, and we can have a child in the future when he is ready."

"See! Now you're thinking straight."

Monica parked, and the two friends walked into the clinic arm in arm. Monica checked in. The receptionist gave her a clipboard and a pen. They sat down in the waiting room, and Monica filled out a brief health questionnaire about the details of her pregnancy. So far the visit was low key and very comfortable. Monica was convinced that she had made the right decision.

A stern-looking nurse appeared in the doorway that led back to the bare-walled procedure rooms. She barked out, "Monica!"

"Yes?" she replied as she rose from her chair. Danni walked back with her to the room. Monica sat down on the end of the exam table between the stirrups. The nurse reviewed the form and sighed audibly, "Ms. Gilbert, we have a problem here."

"What's wrong?" asked Monica.

She looked over her glasses at her and said, "Well, Ms. Gilbert, according to your dates here, your pregnancy is twenty-two weeks along. We handle pregnancies only up to twelve weeks."

"So, what does that mean?" she asked sheepishly.

This nurse intimidated her. She was an older, obviously well-seasoned nurse. Monica wondered if she was all bark and no bite. As if to answer her question, the nurse respectfully responded, "I'm sorry, Monica. It means that you are going to have to go somewhere else to terminate your pregnancy. There is a place about thirty minutes from here that terminates pregnancies that are up to seventeen weeks along. The only clinic that handles pregnancies up to twenty-four weeks is in Chicago."

Monica looked up to the ceiling as if talking to someone up there.

"Chicago! Are you kidding me? I really have to drive to Chicago? Why doesn't anyone around here take care of pregnancies up to twenty-four weeks?"

"The techniques are different. We do suction extractions here. That will not work with an older fetus. It requires a different form of extraction."

"Thank you for your help. This whole thing has been a mess."

"I understand," the nurse kindly replied. She handed Monica a business card from the clinic located on the north side of Chicago.

Danni and Monica got up and walked out of the clinic. As they were walking to the parking lot, the nurse caught up with them. Monica was surprised to see her. The nurse whispered into her ear, "There is another option, Ms. Gilbert. There's a physician here in town who might be able to help you. We are not allowed to refer you officially, but his office is just two blocks east of here." She handed Monica a business card.

"Thanks," she whispered back. "Why are you telling me this?"

"Just trying to help."

The girls got into the car, and Monica told Danni what the nurse had said. Danni responded, "Let's drive by his office and check it out." They found an upscale office building with well-manicured landscaping. A sign in the lawn in front of the building identified the place as the Women's Health Center and the doctor as Hector Johnson, MD.

Monica asked, "Danni, What do you think? Should I go to Chicago or see this Dr. Johnson?"

"I don't know. This is a nice office, and it's convenient. It's a lot closer than Chicago, but why can't they refer you from the clinic? That seems shady. I think I would go to Chicago. What if this local guy, Dr. Johnson, is creepy or a bad physician?"

"Maybe I'll call his office and ask some questions."

Later that day, Monica called and got an appointment for the next day. Danni refused to come with her and warned her not to be alone with the guy.

Doctor Johnson's office was plush and upscale—a far cry from the bare-bones clinic she had gone to the day before. Her visit proceeded as most prenatal visits do. She provided a urine specimen, and the nurse carefully checked her blood pressure and then measured the height of her uterus above the pubic bone. She let Monica listen to the baby's heartbeat with a stethoscope. Suddenly the whole pregnancy thing got real. At her regular obstetrician's office, the nurse listened with a Doppler monitor. Monica had never heard the actual sound of her baby's heart before.

Doctor Johnson was short and round. His jet-black hair was slicked back. He wore scrubs that seemed several sizes too small. He asked Monica many questions, which she answered. "How do you feel about the pregnancy?"

Monica sensed he was fishing for something and responded, "I was excited at first, but now I have decided to have an abortion."

"You're too far along to go to our local clinic."

"So I found out. The nurse there said I would have to go to Chicago."

"She's right. Did she send you here?"

"Yes," she said, "but unofficially."

"I am trained to do abortions. Unfortunately, the hospitals in town have religious affiliations and do not allow elective abortions to be performed. Our local clinic, as you found out, handles only suction extractions, but pregnancies can be terminated due to 'induced spontaneous abortion.'"

"Could you explain that to me in English?" Monica asked.

"Certainly," replied the red faced, slightly embarrassed obstetrician. "You take medications that cause you to go into labor. We wait until the fetus is almost ready to be delivered and have you come to the birthing center. The fetus is delivered there as a stillborn."

"Is it painful?" Monica asked.

"No more than childbirth."

"Is it legal?"

"You can drive to Chicago if you like."

Monica understood what this comment meant. She would deliver a live baby, and they would make sure it did not survive. She told Dr. Johnson that she would think about it, but had already decided that she would go to Chicago. She called Danni to tell her what had happened at Dr. Johnson's office. They agreed that both of them would travel to Chicago.

Later that week, they found themselves in a hotel room on the north side of Chicago. Monica had done a lot of thinking on the trip up and realized she was still on the fence about whether she would proceed with the abortion. She tried to put it out of her mind that night. She and Danni went out to dinner and a show.

The next day, they checked in at a small clinic near their hotel. No one was sitting in the waiting room. Monica and Danni were quickly escorted to a small, plain office. A nurse came in and sat down at the desk. She didn't introduce herself, and Monica never learned her name.

The nurse talked to them in a monotone voice. "Today I will give you some medicine to soften your cervix. This will make the procedure tomorrow much easier to perform."

Monica interrupted, "About the procedure tomorrow, what exactly will the doctor be doing?"

"You will get all that information tomorrow. The doctor will talk to you before the surgery. Your appointment is at eight in the morning in the main clinic. Show up about fifteen minutes early. Here is your health questionnaire. Fill it out completely."

The nurse handed her a clipboard and left the room. Monica diligently completed the medical history questions. The nurse returned and collected the forms. She then told Monica, "Next, our nurse practitioner will examine you and insert some medicine to prepare your cervix for the procedure tomorrow. After the examination, you need to go straight to your hotel room and lie down for two hours. And remember— nothing to eat after midnight."

The next morning they parked the car and walked toward the clinic. Just this short walk from the car almost scared Monica off. Protesters carrying graphic signs and tiny caskets stood on the sidewalk opposite the clinic. Some of the people followed Monica, and one woman ran across the road from the parking lot to the clinic trying to talk to her.

The main clinic was much larger than the one she had visited the day before, and much busier. The waiting room was filled with all kinds of women. Posters about sexually transmitted diseases covered the walls of the waiting area. Literature about birth control was scattered over several tables. The place looked messy and smelled no better. Monica felt out of place. Danni reassured her that everything would be all right. Monica needed this encouragement, especially after her encounter with the protesters.

Just as Monica was ready to get up and walk out of the clinic, she heard her name being called. She looked up and saw a middle-aged, overly tanned woman standing at the doorway leading to the procedure rooms. She shouted, "Ms. Gilbert! Please come with me." Monica and Danni both got up, but the nurse stopped them and allowed only Monica to accompany her beyond the doorway. Danni protested, but the nurse was adamant; it was Monica alone or nobody.

"Why can't Danni come with me?" pleaded Monica.

"Clinic policy," snapped the nurse. "Only the client is allowed in the procedure rooms."

Monica was led down a bare hallway to a white, sterile-smelling room. She was handed a gown to put on and a basket for her belongings, including her smartphone. The nurse collected the basket and sat Monica down in a chair where she stayed for several minutes waiting for the doctor to come in.

A different nurse showed up holding the medical history form Monica had filled out the previous day. This nurse was kind and tried to explain what was about to happen. She felt strongly that women choosing abortion were brave heroes. She explained to Monica, "You will feel some pain when the doctor injects numbing medicine around your cervix. You might feel some discomfort when he dilates your cervix, but hopefully the suppository that was inserted yesterday has done its job. This will minimize the amount of dilation you will need. Once you are dilated, you will feel some tugging and pulling, but no pain."

Monica politely listened to the nurse. Her head was full of questions, concerns, and doubts. She was hoping the doctor could clear some of them up. "Where is the doctor? I need to talk to him."

"The doctor is busy doing a procedure. You will meet him in the surgery room."

"Surgery room? Are you going to put me to sleep?"

"No, this will be a 'local' procedure."

"I have a bunch of questions for him."

The nurse was not used to her clients asking questions. Questions just slowed down the day and caused her to get home late. They were not to be tolerated. She responded just a bit annoyed, "I told you the doctor will talk to you in the surgery room."

Monica didn't like this development. She was used to asking doctors questions. She thought about going back home to Dr. Johnson. The nurse cut off their conversation by giving her a form to sign. It was the consent for surgery. It was chock full of fine print. Monica looked at the form. The words seemed to blur together. She saw one image in her mind—she and Robert were laughing and dancing at the club. This was what she wanted most. Danni's words came to her: "Robert doesn't want to be a father. So, do you want to raise the baby as a single parent?" She thought of the heartbeat she heard at Dr. Johnson's office. Tears streamed down her cheeks and dripped onto the form.

The nurse stood next to her impassively. Tears were common in her business. Pregnant women were emotional creatures. The decision to terminate only heightened their fears. In the end, Monica didn't read the consent, but just signed. She wanted this whole mess to be cleared up. She wanted her boyfriend back. She wanted to go back to the "good old days."

Monica was immediately escorted back to the surgery suite where she climbed up onto a table with stirrups attached. "Where's the doctor?" she asked frantically.

"He'll be here shortly. Hang on." The nurse positioned her in the stirrups and washed her off. She hung a sheet between two poles to block Monica's view.

"Wait a minute," Monica protested. "I want to see what's going on."

"I'm sorry, but we can't do that."

"Why?"

"Clinic policy! You might pass out. We can't have that."

Monica waited impatiently as the nurse arranged a table of instruments. She looked around the darkened room. A bright spotlight was pointed between her legs. As she scanned the room, she happened to catch a glimpse of a reflection in the glass door of a cabinet off to her right side. The door was ajar just enough so Monica could see the nurse at work squirting something out of a syringe.

Suddenly the doctor walked in. He was a tall man with broad shoulders. Monica couldn't see his face because of the surgical scrub hat and mask he wore. Without a word he stepped behind the curtain and started working.

The doctor was behind schedule and needed to catch up. There was no time for idle chatter. These late-term dilation and extractions took longer than his usual suction extractions.

"Hey, I thought you were going to talk to me first," snapped Monica.

"Do you have a question?" returned a stern voice from behind the sheet.

"I want to know what you are going to do to me."

"Didn't the nurse explain it to you?"

"No, she only said it might hurt when you numb me up."

"She was right," he replied. "We are going to place a weighted speculum to expose your cervix." He immediately pushed an instrument into Monica without further warning. "And now you will feel the needle poke."

"Wait!" screamed Monica. "You haven't told me anything yet."

As the needle penetrated Monica he continued, "You will feel burning for a few seconds, and then the pain should disappear."

She jumped a bit, which brought a chorus of, "Hold still!" from both the doctor and the nurse.

After the needle stick, the doctor continued, "I'm going to break your water and then dilate you with some dilators just like we do for D and Cs. I will then evacuate your products of conception."

"Products of conception? What are those?" Monica asked.

"Your fetus and placenta and membranes," quipped the doctor.

"You mean my baby?"

"Well it's not really a baby yet. It's only a mass of tissue. You still have over four months to go before you have a baby." After that comment, he started the procedure. Monica heard a sucking sound first. When that stopped, she felt some pushing and a stretching sensation. She felt discomfort but not really any pain.

Panic was setting in, and Monica was desperate to see what the doctor was doing. She thought about the glass door and looked over to see if she could catch a glimpse of what was happening between her legs. At first she saw the doctor's shoulder and arm. He was wearing a blue paper gown. He leaned over to grab something off a tray. She was shocked to see his hand return holding a really long and very large clamp. This he inserted into her body. He pulled back the clamp forcefully. She felt something like a cramp in her belly. A tiny pair of legs appeared, and then the lower part of the body. They were covered in a white slimy film. She could see the baby struggling and squirming. The doctor cursed out loud.

Monica found herself squirming and kicking as if she was also trying to escape the doctor's grip. Both doctor and nurse as one yelled, "Hold still!"

The doctor continued, "We're almost done. Please try to be patient and relax. It will be over soon."

The next steps of the procedure followed very quickly. Monica gasped and closed her eyes tightly like a two-year-old pretending this was not happening. She wiped back tears, which were welling up in her eyes. She wanted to scream 'Stop!' but couldn't. The words stuck in her throat.

The baby suddenly stopped moving and was quickly removed in pieces. Finally, the uterus was scraped to make sure no traces were retained. The nurse tossed the pieces of Monica's baby and placenta into a tray on a nearby table awaiting the doctor's inspection.

It was over. Her baby was gone. She wondered if it had been a boy or girl. She wondered what color hair it had and the color of its eyes. She wondered if it looked like her or Robert. She suddenly wished that she could hold her baby in her arms. Why had she agreed to this procedure?

Monica regained her composure and blurted out, "Was it a boy or a girl?"

"We couldn't tell," answered the nurse, "The fetus was too small."

"What do you mean small? It looked pretty big to me."

The startled doctor peeked up over the sheet and demanded, "How do you know how big the fetus was? This sheet blocked your view."

"I saw it in the glass door," admitted Monica, pointing to the cabinet.

The horrified doctor angrily scolded the nurse, "That door is supposed to be closed!"

"I—I'm sorry," stammered the nurse. "I didn't realize it was open."

The doctor quickly finished his work. He walked around to the side of the examination table and sat down beside Monica. He dropped his mask revealing deep wrinkles etched into his face and a bushy moustache. He asked in a rather harsh tone, "What all did you see?"

"I saw legs and a body. I saw my baby squirming. Do you think it felt any pain?"

The doctor's attitude softened, "Ms. Gilbert, let me explain something to you. Your fetus was not fully developed. At twenty-three weeks gestational age, it cannot think and has no clue what's going on around it. It cannot feel pain. The actions you saw were merely primitive reflexes."

"Oh, thank God," Monica said with a sigh. The doctor's words consoled her. Certainly, if the brain and feeling of pain weren't developed yet, her baby hadn't suffered.

This relief, however, was short lived. She had seen glimpses of a horrific scene. Over the next few weeks, images of the little legs and squirming slimy body, and the pieces of bloody placenta and baby being thrown into the tray on the table crept into her dreams at night and thoughts during the day.

The weeks following her procedure were catastrophic for Monica. She became depressed and moody. She couldn't help it. Tears and uncontrollable sobbing came upon her without warning. Her family physician gave her antidepressants and diagnosed her with post-traumatic stress syndrome. At times she wanted to get pregnant again and have a dozen babies to make up for the one she gave up. At other times, she felt so guilty that she believed she didn't deserve to have any children.

She went out with Robert several times after the abortion. One evening, they were sitting in the same restaurant where Robert had announced his plan for them to live together. "Monica," Robert began in a rather mournful tone, "we have been together for a long time. We've been through so much. I love you very much, but we can't go on like this."

Monica burst into tears, "Are we breaking up?"

"Yes," replied Robert his voice shaking, "We are."

"But why?"

"You are never happy anymore. We used to be so good for each other. That has all changed. Now you're always depressed, and I'm always upset."

"Let me get this straight," she angrily interrupted. "I gave up my baby for you, and now you're dumping me?" She felt betrayed. Robert was supposed to understand more than anyone how she was feeling, but now he was plunging a knife into her back.

"It's not like that. I'm not 'dumping' you. We are parting as friends."

Monica got up out of her seat, grabbed her purse, and stormed out of the restaurant muttering, "It sure feels like I'm being dumped. Some friend you are."

Everyone was betraying her. First Danni had stopped talking to her. Monica apparently was making her best friend depressed with her endless stream of tears and their conversations about the abortion.

That was the last time Monica ever saw Robert. He took a new job and moved to the East Coast. She still loved him. It hurt to think about it. It hurt to think about losing her baby. The hardest part for her was seeing children at the playground. They brought up such painful memories and emotions. For a while Monica avoided any place where she might run into a child. Eventually she got over the grief and wanted to be around children. Walking around at the shopping mall was therapeutic for her. She could watch families interact, yet keep her distance.

# Allison

Monica was horrified when Julie told her how much Allison had suffered at twenty-three weeks gestational age. Monica buried her face in her hands and wept bitterly for the pain she now knew she had caused her own baby. The image of the little legs and body squirming in the clamp played in her mind. She recalled the pieces of her baby carelessly tossed away into the stainless steel tray. Before learning about Allison, she had not realized that she had been the cause of such pain. The doctor in Chicago had flat-out lied to her. The grief came in waves and reduced Monica to incoherence.

Julie sat quietly, still not understanding why this stranger sat weeping and wailing next to her. She waited patiently for Monica to spend all her tears.

Monica softened, and her wailing faded to quiet sobs. Finally, she regained her composure and poured out her bitter tale while Julie did her best to comfort her. They talked for almost two hours.

Julie explained that, when her baby was sick to the point of death, she found strength and hope from a poem written centuries ago by a king who despaired for his life. She recited the poem for Monica:

> The Lord is my shepherd,
> I shall not be in want.
> He makes me lie down in green pastures,
> He leads me beside quiet waters,
> He restores my soul.
> He guides me in paths of righteousness
> For his name's sake.
> Even though I walk through the valley
> Of the shadow of Death,
> I will fear no evil,
> For you are with me;

Your rod and staff,
They comfort me.
You prepare a table before me
In the presence of my enemies.
My cup overflows.
Surely goodness and love will follow me
All the days of my life,
And I will dwell in the house of the Lord
Forever. (Psalm 23 New International Version 1984)

Monica nodded, acknowledging that she knew the poem. She said to Julie, "I know this poem. My grandma has a sampler on her wall with those words on it, and a shepherd and sheep on a hill stitched underneath them, but what does it mean?"

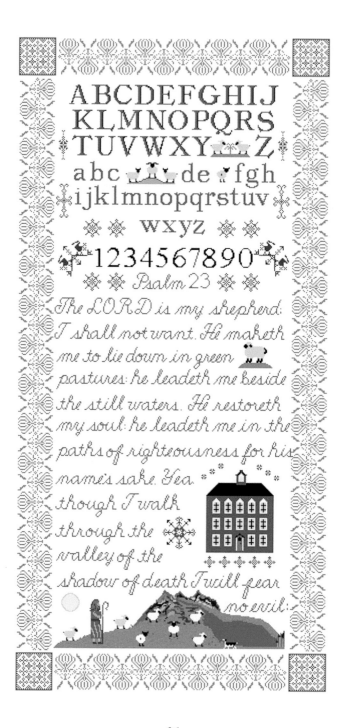

ABCDEFGHIJ
KLMNOPQRS
TUVWXY Z
abc de fgh
ijklmnopqrstuv
✳ ✳ ✳ wxyz ✳ ✳ ✳
1234567890
✳ ✳ Psalm 23 ✳ ✳

The LORD is my shepherd:
I shall not want. He maketh
me to lie down in green
pastures: he leadeth me beside
the still waters. He restoreth
my soul: he leadeth me in the
paths of righteousness for his
name's sake. Yea,
though I walk
through the
valley of the
shadow of death I will fear
no evil:

Julie replied, "The poem describes the relationship I have with the God who created me. He created you too, you know. We are the sheep in the poem. He is the shepherd responsible for caring for us, providing for our needs, and protecting us. Just as a shepherd leads his sheep to food and water, he leads us to a place of peace and rest. He takes us down the right paths. Just as a shepherd uses his staff to protect and guide his sheep, God leads us through tough places. Even when we are scared to death, he is with us to comfort us. We truly don't have to fear any evil. Our shepherd anoints our heads with oil to keep us healthy just as a shepherd covers his sheep with oil to rid them of bugs and ticks. God provides for us so generously that our cups are always full and overflowing. God relentlessly pursues us with his love and goodness. He prepares a place for us to be with him for all eternity."

Monica replied, "Wow, I never realized there was someone looking out for me."

"There is, Monica. He is the one who saved my little Allie. He is the one who kept me from despair when Allie was sick. He is the one who kept me and my husband together through this ordeal. He will be there for you too, if you want him."

"I don't know about that," Monica replied. "But I do want to hear more about your God."

Allie had slept the entire time Julie and Monica conversed, but she finally awoke hungry for food. Julie allowed Monica to hold her baby and give her a bottle. Monica smiled for the first time in weeks. This was not her baby, but Allie somehow touched and satisfied a deep maternal instinct Monica had been fighting hard to suppress.

They agreed to meet in two days at Julie's Bible study for young moms. She wanted to introduce Monica to her close friends and help her deal with her tragedy. She called Bill at his office and told him about the chance meeting. Later that night, in their dining room over supper, she gave him a full accounting of the crazy day she'd had.

"I can't believe Monica believed the lies that doctor was peddling," Julie told her husband. "She must be weak and gullible. The funny thing is that she came across to me as strong and independent."

"Don't be too harsh on her. Who knows how you would react if you were thrown into her situation?"

"I know that, but who would allow someone to kill the baby you had been carrying for months. That seems cold and heartless."

"Yeah but you and I desperately wanted Allie. Robert rejected his child from the beginning. Monica held on to hope until it evaporated, and her friend Danni certainly didn't help to save the baby."

"I suppose she gave up all hope and felt abortion was the only option. Do you think that sort of thing happens a lot?"

"I don't know for sure, but I suspect it does."

"What is it that drives strong, independent, and intelligent women to abort their babies?"

"Probably convenience, but I imagine that fear and despair also play a role."

"That was certainly true for Monica."

"So how do we help Monica?"

"I invited her to my moms' group."

"Do you think that's wise?"

"I think being with moms and babies will help her heal."

"How about Doc Newberry?"

"What about him?"

"I can ask him to talk with her, maybe interpret what she saw and help her deal with it. He comes to that men's group I attend on the first Saturday morning of each month. We've become good friends."

When Monica first went to Julie's moms' group meeting, she felt out of place in a room full of moms and babies and young children. When the moms learned what had happened to her, however, they opened their arms and accepted her. A real breakthrough happened when Monica was asked to take care of a young baby for an entire weekend while one of the moms went on a trip with her husband. Julie, of course, offered to step in and help if things got crazy.

Julie eventually suggested to Monica that she should see Dr. Newberry and talk to him about her experience. He knew premies well and could probably help her interpret the things she had seen.

In a few weeks' time, Monica met Dr. Newberry in his office. His nurse also sat in on the meeting, which took place in a conference room with a large mahogany table and overstuffed leather side chairs. They sat together at one end of the table.

"Monica, I am Dr. Newberry, and this is my nurse Abigail."

"Abby," said Abigail as she reached out to shake Monica's hand.

"We have lots of experience with very small babies, as you already know from Julie. She told me the basics of your story, but I wanted to hear it directly from you."

Monica replied, "So where do I start?"

"How about starting when you went into the surgery room."

"Okay. The nurse led me down a long hallway to the surgery room. She opened the door and showed me a table to sit on. It was padded and comfortable. There were stirrups at the end. I was wearing one of those flimsy gowns. The nurse helped me into the stirrups and scooted my bottom down to the end of the bed."

"That all sounds pretty normal for any obstetrical procedure," responded Dr. Newberry. "The stirrups allow the obstetrician to get between your legs and have easy access to the baby."

"Everything was fine until the nurse raised each of the stirrups high in the air. It made my hips hurt. I felt like a wishbone getting pulled apart. The nurse hung a drape between me and the instruments and stuff. The doctor came in and sat on a roll-around chair. I assume Julie told you I saw the whole thing in the glass door of the cabinet."

"Yes, she did tell me."

"He then rolled up to the table and the nurse assisted him. He stood up and put on a paper gown and gloves. He sat back down and pushed a weighted something into me."

"It was a speculum to expose your cervix."

"Yes, that is what he said. He then took a syringe and needle and stabbed me several times. It burned at first and then went numb."

"He did what is called a paracervical block. It numbs your cervix so he could dilate it with little pain. Did you get any gel inserted the day before?"

"No it was a giant tampon-like thing."

"That was a hormone called dinoprostone. It's a prostaglandin suppository that softens your cervix the way it softens on its own when you are in labor."

"He must have sucked out my water because I heard a sucking sound. I then felt pressure like being stretched."

"He was using Hegar dilators to stretch out your cervix. Once it was big enough, he should have been able to pull out your baby's feet."

"Yeah, I saw them. The doctor grabbed them with a giant clamp thing, but the baby squirmed. I think it was fighting back. I felt something in my belly."

"Are you sure you want to continue? The next part is going to get gruesome."

"I want to go on. I have some questions."

"What happened next?"

"I saw that the body and legs were covered with white slimy stuff."

"That is called vernix caseosa. It coats the baby's skin. It gets absorbed as the pregnancy progresses. Premature babies have thick white coats."

"The doctor was pulling very hard, and when the legs and body appeared, he cursed. Why would he curse?"

"I don't think he intended to pull the baby out. He was using a Sopher clamp. Some people call them long ring forceps. We use them in surgery to break up organs like the spleen in order to remove them laparoscopically. We break up a big organ and pull it out in pieces through a little hole. He probably was intending to pull pieces out, not the whole baby."

"That is horrible," said Monica, now visibly shaken.

"We can stop anytime," replied Dr. Newberry in a soothing and reassuring tone.

Doctor Newberry's nurse, who had been silent and almost motionless up to this point, got up and walked to Monica's side of the table. She offered her a box of tissues while placing a comforting hand on her shoulder. Monica blew her nose and sighed. Having pulled herself together she said, "I'm okay. Let's go on."

"Did you see what the doctor did to your baby after that?"

"No, I closed my eyes, and when I opened them the doctor's body blocked the view. My baby stopped moving. Before that, I could feel the baby struggling in the birth canal, but it suddenly stopped. That's when I knew ..." Monica began sobbing. Between sobs she wailed, "Then I saw the pieces being thrown onto the tray." The nurse now sat down beside her and put her arm around her. The tears continued for a long time.

Monica had not realized that the scar created by her "pregnancy termination" had followed her into every aspect of her life. Her meeting with Dr. Newberry and his compassionate nurse proved transformative. She told Julie all about the meeting the next time they met for coffee.

Julie asked her, "How did it make you feel when Dr. Newberry had you describe the abortion?"

"It was the worst thing I have ever had to do, but it was necessary. I'm glad you recommended him. He and his nurse, Abby, are about the most compassionate people I have ever met."

"They are very special to me. I wouldn't have Allie without them. "In fact," Julie said, "Doctor Newberry once told me that God saved Allie's life, not him. God worked through *his* hands."

"I have never thought about God working through a person."

"My pastor says we are God's hands and feet. He works through us to accomplish what he wants."

It was through discussions like this that Monica found her way to forgiveness from God. She spent many hours in prayer and in Bible study with Julie. She slowly began living again. She and Julie remained close friends, sharing little Allie even after Monica married, became pregnant, and delivered her own precious little girl. She named her Julie Allison in honor of the two women who helped her move from death into life, to find hope behind her tears.

# Afterword

This book is based on the real experiences of real people. Julie's story is a tale of tragedy and despair turned into hope and deliverance. Thousands of premies all over the world are being saved through developments in technology and patient care. The lowest gestational age at which babies can survive now is twenty-one to twenty-two weeks. Few at these ages survive due to complications of their prematurity. Babies born at twenty-three weeks, however, now do survive. In some neonatal intensive care units, over half these babies survive to be discharged from the hospital. Allison is one of the extremely premature babies to benefit from the development of surfactant for the lungs. Surfactant is a soapy fluid made by the lung to help the air sacs stay open during breathing. Without surfactant, the air sacs collapse and lose their ability to transfer oxygen to the blood. Before surfactant was available, babies under the age of twenty-five weeks rarely survived. Babies born at twenty-three and twenty-four weeks were considered not viable; they were allowed to die. Now these babies routinely survive. With further developments, who knows what will happen? Maybe we will figure out how to make an artificial womb to grow all premies up to viable ages.

The one thing we have learned from keeping ever-smaller babies alive is that they have their own personalities, even at twenty-three weeks. They respond, in many ways, the same as older, more mature babies. Pain perception and response is one of these areas. Even the late first and early second trimester babies feel pain and respond to it. With the advent of advanced ultrasound used for procedures like in-utero (while the baby is still in the uterus) bladder aspiration, we can see even fourteen- to seventeen-week fetuses reacting and trying to avoid the needle when it penetrates the bladder.

Monica's story is a sad tale of mistakes and deception. Monica thought she would be better off without her baby, but found out only too late that she had been wrong. The nurses and doctors at the clinic kept telling Monica that her "fetus" or "products of conception" comprised a lifeless, shapeless piece of tissue almost like a tumor that needed to be removed. In fact, Monica's baby and thousands just like hers was a viable, healthy baby who felt pain just like you and I.

Monica saw what happens below the sheet that separates abortionist and mother. Few women have the chance to see what is done to their babies. If that veil was torn away and the truth revealed, most women would shudder at the horror awaiting them. Monica's baby was killed in cold blood during a procedure called dilation and extraction. It was tortured, killed, and then discarded under the banner of reproductive freedom and women's choice. It suffered no less pain than you and I would if someone took a pair of large pliers and crushed our legs, and then, while we struggled to free ourselves, started hacking our bodies apart. This sounds like a scene from a Hollywood horror film about the acts of a serial killer, but it happens in clinics in cities all around us.

If physicians carried out research projects involving any type of animal and performed this same procedure, the project would be shut down and canceled as *unethical*. The physicians would be labeled guilty of cruelty to animals in their research and would certainly face sanctions. Dogs and rats in our society have more rights than unborn human babies. It is time to do something about it. Abortion is very simply a barbaric and inhuman practice. I shudder to think of the pain and suffering foisted upon defenseless, unborn premies. Do not believe the lie that fetuses don't feel pain. They do! I know because I am a pediatric surgeon who has operated on many little Allisons. I owe it to these precious little lives to get the truth out.

Monica found forgiveness and restoration through a friend who offered her the truth in love. That truth is that God loves us even when we mess up—even if we participate in the termination of a perfect little life. There are many people who will offer you the truth without judgment. All around the world, Hope Pregnancy Centers offer counseling for pregnant women, but also counseling for post-abortion women. If you need forgiveness and hope, call one of these centers.

# About the Author

Dr. Smith is a busy pediatric surgeon in Fort Wayne, IN. He lives with his wife Carolyn who helps him run his practice. He has cared for thousands of children during his years as a surgeon. He considers each and every one of his patients to be like one his own children. His 'kids' are very special and he loves all of them.

Printed in the United States
By Bookmasters